Ballet

Julie Haydon

Chapter 1

What Is a Ballet?

A ballet is a story told with dance and music. The story is told without words.

The dancers wear **costumes** and make-up.
They dance on a stage.
The stage can be made
to look like different places.

A ballet can be funny, sad or exciting. Many ballets tell stories about people and animals.

a goose

Some ballets tell **fairy tales** and other stories from books.

Cinderella

Sometimes a ballet does not tell a story. A ballet can be about how people feel or it can just have movement and music.

Chapter 2

Learning Ballet

Many children learn ballet.
Ballet is fun.
It can help children to be fit and strong.

At ballet classes, children learn ballet steps and how to move to music.

Older boys and girls
learn how to dance together.
The girls learn how to dance
on the tips of their toes
in special ballet shoes.

Ballet students learn how to use their faces and bodies to tell a story without words.

Most ballet schools put on shows. The ballet students dance in the shows in front of their families and friends.

Chapter 3

A Ballet Company

Some ballet students grow up and get work as ballet dancers. Ballet dancers work for a **ballet company**.

A ballet company puts on ballets in **theatres.** People pay money to see the ballets.

Ballet dancers are not the only people in a ballet company.
It takes lots of different people to put on a ballet.

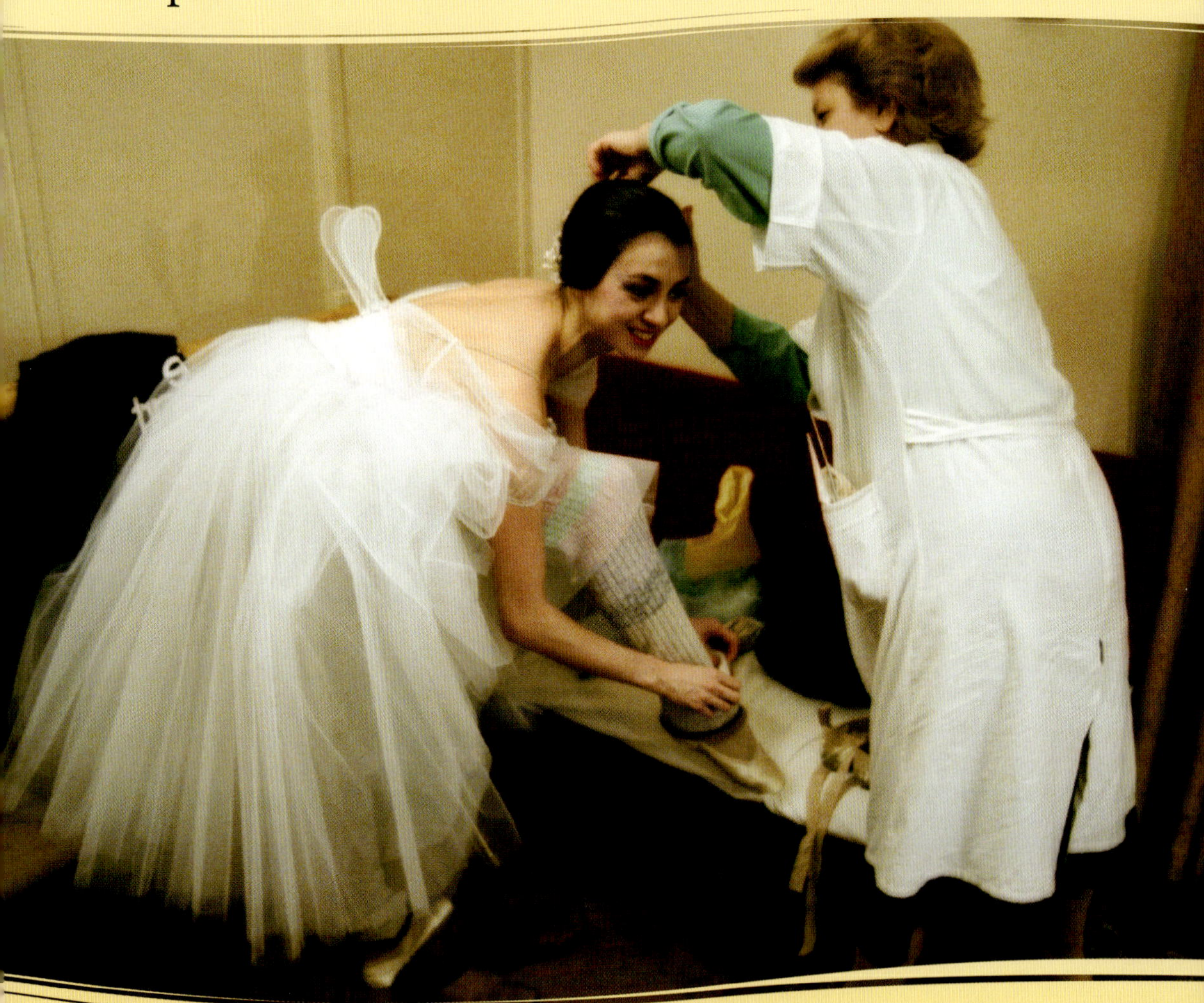

Chapter 4

Putting on a Ballet

This is how a ballet company puts on a ballet.

The head of the ballet company chooses the ballet.

Sometimes the head of the ballet company asks for a new ballet to be made. A new ballet needs a story and new steps.

A new ballet might need new music too.

The dancers learn the steps and how to dance them to music.

Costumes are made for the dancers to wear. Dancers wear out lots of ballet shoes, so **spare** shoes are needed.

The stage is set.
Everything on the stage must be easy to move on and off quickly.
The lights are set up.

The dancers practise and practise.
The musicians practise and practise.

Tickets for the ballet go on sale.

Chapter 5

Opening Night

It is the **opening night** of the ballet.
The theatre is full of people.
The lights go down.

The music starts.

The curtain goes up.
The stage looks wonderful.
The dancers start to dance.

At the end of the ballet,
the **audience** claps.
Everyone at the ballet company
feels very happy.
All the hard work has been worth it!

Glossary

audience	the people who watch a ballet
ballet company	a group of people who put on ballets
costumes	special clothes that dancers wear
fairy tales	very old stories about people and magic
opening night	the first night a ballet is performed
spare	extra, more
theatres	buildings where ballets are performed

Index